HUBBLE·BUBBLE

The WACKY WINTER WONDERLAND!

TRACEY CORDEROY

JOE BERGER

nosy
crow

First published in the UK in 2015 by Nosy Crow Ltd
The Crow's Nest, 10a Lant Street
London, SE1 1QR, UK

Nosy Crow and associated logos are trademarks and/or registered
trademarks of Nosy Crow Ltd

Text copyright © Tracey Corderoy, 2015
Cover and illustrations copyright © Joe Berger, 2015

The right of Tracey Corderoy and Joe Berger to be identified
as the author and illustrator respectively of this work has been asserted
by them in accordance with the Copyright, Designs
and Patents Act 1988.

1 3 5 7 9 10 8 6 4 2

A CIP catalogue record for this book will be available from the British Library.

Printed in Italy by Imago

Papers used by Nosy Crow are made from wood grown in
sustainable forests.

ISBN: 978 0 85763 494 8

www.nosycrow.com

CONTENTS

There was nothing Pandora loved more than spending time with her granny. Araminta Violet Crow was exciting, funny and kind. The only tiny problem was you never quite knew what she'd get up to next. You see, Pandora's granny was (whisper this next bit) … *a witch.*

The WACKY WINTER WONDERLAND!

Chapter One

"Oooh, Granny!" Pandora cried. "Can I try one of your biscuits?"

"Of course!" smiled Granny. "But wait a moment and I'll ice them!"

It was Christmas Eve and Granny was at Pandora's house doing "Christmassy" things. Pandora had just made a snowflake paper-chain, while Granny had baked gingerbread snowmen biscuits.

Granny waved her wand and with a small
– *pop!* – the biscuits were all beautifully
iced.

She then took some small glass jars
from her cauldron filled with sweets and
sprinkles.

"These are *magical* sweets," Granny
said, giving each little snowman a row of
gumdrop buttons and a black liquorice
top-hat.

"*How* are they magical?" Pandora asked.
But Granny just winked. "You'll see!"

With that, Pandora's parents arrived home. They'd been out doing last-minute Christmas shopping.

"Mmmm – *gingerbread*!" Pandora's dad smiled.

"My favourite!" nodded her mum.

Granny offered them a magical biscuit and they each took a bite. Pandora watched to see what would happen next...

"Oh!" said her dad as he started to chew. "Those gumdrops are fizzing on my tongue!"

"Mine too!" giggled her mum. "So tickly!"

They both swallowed. And then, in a puff of magic snowflakes, Pandora's dad turned into a *snowman*! By his side was a snow-woman wearing a headband of snowdrops … and a frown.

Pandora gasped. "Mum? Dad?"

"Surprise!" called Granny. "*That's* what the magic sweets do!"

Pandora looked worried.

"It's all right," Granny said. "It was just a bit of fun. Watch this!"

With a swish of her wand, the snow melted away to reveal Pandora's parents underneath it.

They were wet. And they didn't look happy with Granny at all…

"No more m-a-g-i-c!" puffed Hugo, dripping on to the carpet.

"Not for the rest of the day," Moonbeam added icily. She sighed. "Now, isn't it time you were going?"

"Good heavens!" beamed Granny, checking the clock. "You're right!"

Granny was taking Pandora to a nearby farm which had been turned into a Winter Wonderland. There was going to be a sparkly ice-rink, jolly elves and yummy Christmas food. There was *even* a magical sleigh ride to see Santa!

Pandora clapped her hands.

"Hooray!" she cheered. She'd been looking forward to this FOR AGES.

Granny whistled for her broomstick and they both jumped on.

"Full speed ahead!" cried Pandora.

14

Chapter
Two

But when they arrived at the Winter
Wonderland, Pandora's face fell.

The thin, patchy snow smelled like
shaving-foam, the farmyard was dotted
with horse-poo, and the farmer selling
tickets looked really *cross*...

"That cat can't come in for a start!"
he puffed, glowering at Cobweb.

"But it's a *farm*," replied Granny.

"Huh!" barked the farmer. "Well, you'll need to buy a ticket for him, too!"

Granny paid then they marched away to explore. There were crowds of people but they all looked glum. This place was really *horrid*.

The shaving-foam snow was all sticky and yuck. And it made poor Cobweb sneeze!

And the ice-rink wasn't *real* ice either –
just mucky sheets of bubble-wrap stuck
together.

"Want to skate?" growled a grumpy-looking elf, waving a pair of grubby ice-skates.

"Hang on…" said Pandora. It was *Rory* – a Year 6 boy from her school. His friend, Ben, stood beside him in a hat with a bell, scowling.

"You're not elves!" Pandora said.

"Are SO!" Rory glowered. Then he lowered his voice so Granny couldn't hear. "And say that again and we'll tell *Santa* you've been BAD!"

"And you know what that will mean," Ben glared. "No PRESSIES!"

With that, Pandora spied Nellie and Jake standing outside the Festive Food Hall with Jake's dad. She hurried Granny over, pleased to have found some friends!

The Festive Food Hall was just a damp, old tent. The "festive food" was disappointing too…

"Want my sprouts?" groaned Jake.

"No thanks!" Pandora shuddered.

"How about my mug of cold tea?" said Nellie with a sigh.

With that, Farmer Grumpypants appeared, leading Santa's "reindeers" through the yard.

"Those aren't reindeers!" grumbled Jake. "They're *dogs* with antlers on their heads!"

Pandora sighed. "I wish they *were* reindeers…"

"Maybe they can be?" whispered Granny, edging out her wand.

"Better not," said Pandora. "The farmer might get even crosser."

They watched as the dogs were led into a barn where a pig trough on pram wheels stood waiting.

"Oh no!" gasped Pandora. "Is *that* the sleigh that takes you on the magical ride to Santa?"

She looked at Granny, almost in tears. But Granny's eyes were twinkling. And as soon as the farmer closed the barn door behind him, Granny flicked her wand at the fake ice-rink and it turned into a real one instead! With another quick wand-flick, the children's poo-splattered wellies became the *sparkliest* ice-skates.

"Even *Cobweb's* got some!" Pandora giggled, as Granny launched him on to the ice…

"Wheeee!"

Chapter Three

Ice-skating was great!

Pandora went slowly, but *Granny* leaped and spun. *"Beep beep!"* she called as she weaved through the crowds. "Such fun!"

After their skating, everyone felt peckish so Granny magicked up some *real* festive food. Gone were the mugs of stone-cold tea. Instead they had yummy hot chocolate

with marshmallows, and cupcakes
decorated like reindeers.

"*Mmmm,*" said the children,
tucking in. "Thanks, Granny!"

When it got dark, they trekked
across the fields to see the
Twinkling Tunnel of Lights.
But they needn't have bothered –
because, when they got there…

"*Oh no!*" the children sighed. The **Twinkling Tunnel** was just two bare trees with some lightbulbs strung between them.

"*Really!*" spluttered Granny. "Leave this to me!" She pointed her wand at the trees and trilled…

"Out with winter trees so bare – and in with **TWINKLES** everywhere!"

Whoosh – a stream of sparkles burst from her wand and hit the bare trees full-force. At once they began sprouting big, green leaves.

28

Then, climbing roses sprang
from the earth, curling up the
tree trunks and arching over to
make the most *magical* tunnel.

"And look!" cried Pandora,
as hundreds of fairy lights
twinkled among the roses.

But suddenly a little cluster of lights *flew off*.

Pandora looked more closely.

Wait – the fairy lights weren't *lights* at all but real *fairies* with rainbow-coloured wings!

More and more fairies fluttered off to play. Some were graceful while others were little acrobats. And one bunch was really quite *cheeky*…

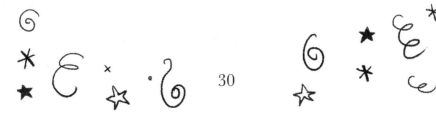

"Wheee!" They showered the children in petals they'd just tugged off the bushes. Then one naughty fairy snatched Granny's wand and zoomed out of reach. "Hee hee!"

"Hey! No!" spluttered Granny. "Give me back my wand!" But the fairy just poked her tongue out at her!

She flicked Granny's wand – and to her delight, magic *snowflakes* puffed out of the end.

"Oooooooh!" grinned the fairy, and she flicked the wand again.

And again,

and again,

and again!

In no time all, a small blizzard was raging as everyone dived for the wand.

Then all of a sudden Jake cried,
"*Someone's coming!*" And everyone peered
through the snowstorm.

"Oh no!" Pandora gave a little squeak.
"It's Farmer Grumpypants!"

Chapter Four

"Who's snowing in my field?" the farmer boomed, battling through the magical storm.

Gasping, the fairy dropped the wand and Granny snatched it up.

"Quick, everyone!" she cried as the farmer got closer. "Follow me!"

Turning, Granny raced off through the field and everyone dashed behind.

As they ran, Nellie saw that the magical snow had stopped, but the sky was still filled with fluffy white things.

"Look, Pandora!" she called, and Pandora looked up...

"It's *really* snowing!"

They followed Granny through the snow-covered fields as tiny stars now winked in the sky. But the farmer was catching up.

"Aha!" said Granny. She knew *just* the thing. With a flick of her wand, they were all wearing *skis*. "He'll never catch us now!" she smiled.

The wind whistled through their hair
as they skied uphill and down. They flew
past the ice-rink which twinkled in the
moonlight. The smell of hot chocolate still
hung in the air and the trees were all fluffy
with snow.

"It looks *so* pretty now!" Pandora smiled.

Granny then led them across the farmyard, where any stray horse-poo was now buried DEEP beneath a thick blanket of snow.

"In here!" she cried, pulling open the big barn door.

Inside the "reindeers" were all snoozing. But their eyes opened wide at the sight of Granny and their ears pricked up at once.

"Ah, yes," smiled Granny as their tails started wagging. "You're ready for an *adventure*. Me too!"

She waved her wand and – **whizz-pop!** – the old pig trough turned into the most *beautiful* sleigh decorated with holly, and ivy, and red and white candy-canes.

Granny put harnesses on the dogs, who looked *very* excited. Then she hurried everyone into the sleigh and quickly took up the reins.

"But those reindeers are *dogs*," said Nellie. "They can't *fly*!"

"They can now!" Pandora grinned. And
she waved her *own* wand at the dogs…

"Take us on a magical sleigh ride!" she
called. "Izzy-wizzy-otious!"

Pandora's spell did the trick beautifully.
The dogs trotted out through the open door
and the sleigh slowly lifted off the ground.

But the farmer was coming through the yard. "Oh, no you don't!" he called at them, waving Granny's broomstick in the air.

"Oh, yes we do!" Granny grinned back. And as the sleigh whooshed over his head, she leaned out and grabbed her broomstick.

"Happy Christmas!" she chuckled as they zoomed away – up, and up, and up!

Pandora had never had such a *magical*
ride. Not even on Granny's broomstick!
Soon they were soaring past a huge silver
moon, looking down on beautiful snowy
rooftops.

Pandora snuggled up with her friends.
As Winter Wonderlands went, this had
to be the most wacky and *wonderful* EVER!

BEST
IN
SHOW!

Chapter One

Pandora was at Granny's house getting
Cobweb ready for a pet show in the Town
Hall. All the pets had to look their *very*
best *and* have a special talent.
Cobweb was nervously waiting
for his bath.

"Now, which bubble-bath
shall we use?" asked Granny.

"Um…" said Pandora.

Granny's bathroom was full of "special" lotions and potions.

"Aha!" said Granny, picking up a bottle. **"Candyfloss Surprise!** Perfect!"

Granny poured the red potion into Cobweb's bathwater. The water fizzed then turned bright pink.

Carefully, Granny popped Cobweb in and Pandora helped to wash him. Then they rinsed off the bubbles and Granny started drying him with her hairdryer.

All was going well, until – suddenly – **doingggggg!** Cobweb's silky black fur had turned shocking pink and fluffed out

like candyfloss!

"Arggh!" shrieked Granny. "Silly me! I forgot – Candyfloss Surprise sometimes *does* that."

"But how can we fix it?" Pandora cried. "He can't enter the pet show like that!"

Granny thought for a moment. Then she waved her wand over Cobweb's fluffed-out fur. With a magical – pop! – the pink fuzziness vanished, and Cobweb was back to normal.

"And look!" smiled Pandora. She had found a blackcurrant-smelling pamper-mitt.

Pandora sat Cobweb beside her on the sofa and rubbed the mitt softly down his back.

"Goodness!" smiled Granny. It made his fur shine a treat!

Cobweb's special talent was tightrope-walking and trapeze. Granny had rigged up a tightrope in the garden and a trapeze-swing hanging off the tree. They took Cobweb out for one last practice before they had to head to the show.

"That's the way, Cobweb!" Pandora smiled as the little black cat glided across the tightrope without a wibble or wobble in sight. "I think he might even win the show."

"Best *get* him there, then!" Granny nodded. She whistled for her broomstick.

"Off we go!"

Chapter
Two

The pavement outside the Town Hall was *heaving* with talented pets as Pandora and Granny joined the queue.

Pandora eyed-up the competition. There was a dancing dog, a helter-skeltering snail, and EVEN a singing goldfish!

"He can sing *opera*," his owner boasted to Pandora.

Granny looked worried. "These pets are

REALLY clever."

"Well, Cobweb is clever too!" Pandora
smiled.

They all went inside, gave details about
their pets, then lined them up ready for
Round One. This round was called Bright
Eyes and Bushy Tails! And the judges
were looking for well-groomed, healthy-
looking pets.

Two judges walked along the line examining each pet in turn. One of them reminded Pandora of a stick insect – he was so tall and thin. And the other (who looked like a pug) was saying such *sniffy* things…

"I don't like the look of your goldfish's poop!"

"That dog has mud on its nose…"

"Eww – your snail is leaving slime-trails *everywhere*!"

Finally they stopped at Cobweb who was sitting in Granny's arms. Cobweb's black coat looked as soft as velvet.

"So *shiny*," the thin judge nodded.

Granny nudged Pandora and gave a little wink. "As shiny as a blackcurrant!" she whispered. "Thanks to you!"

The lady judge checked Cobweb's eyes. Then his ears, nose and tail.

"A nice long tail," she said, and Granny beamed.

The judges wrote a few things down, then moved along the line. When the pets had all been checked the judges went out to award their points in private. When they came back, Round Two would begin. This round was called Clever Clogs! where the pets would show off their special talents.

While everyone waited for the judges to come back, Granny magicked up a tightrope for Cobweb to walk across later. Then she joined all the other contestants for a drink.

Cobweb had a lovely saucer of milk, while Granny and Pandora both chose milkshakes. Granny used her wand to give them extra froth and sprinkles! Pandora was just finishing hers off when a little boy behind yelled... "MUM!"

His guinea-pig had wandered into
another pet's carrying-case, and somehow
the door had jammed shut.

"Open the door!" the little boy shouted.
"MUM!"

His mother dashed over and gave the
door a tug. But it wouldn't budge an inch.

"Yoo hoo!" waved Granny.
"Maybe *I* could help?"

She jumped to her feet, her
wand in the air. "Stand
back!"

"Granny – no – stop!" Pandora gasped.
"Un-jamming spells are so tricky!"

"Not for me, dear!" Granny smiled.
"Watch this!"

She tapped the case door with her wand
and uttered the spell, "Open-up-i-o!"

The door gave a twitch. But stayed firmly
shut.

"Hmm…" said Granny. "This calls for

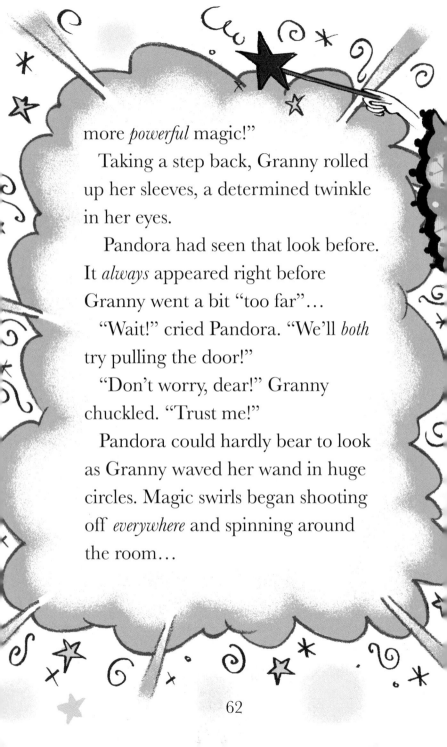

more *powerful* magic!"

Taking a step back, Granny rolled up her sleeves, a determined twinkle in her eyes.

Pandora had seen that look before. It *always* appeared right before Granny went a bit "too far"…

"Wait!" cried Pandora. "We'll *both* try pulling the door!"

"Don't worry, dear!" Granny chuckled. "Trust me!"

Pandora could hardly bear to look as Granny waved her wand in huge circles. Magic swirls began shooting off *everywhere* and spinning around the room…

Ping!
ping!
ping! – they hit the carrying-case and the door sprang open at once.

"There – you see!" Granny said with a smile.

"But look!" gasped Pandora. The magical swirls were pinging off the *pets* now too!

"Um – don't worry!" said Granny, looking worried. "I … oooo…"

With that, the swirls faded and vanished from sight. And for a moment all seemed well. Then a teeny-tiny kitten opened its teeny-tiny mouth and…

"Woof!"

But that wasn't all. The donkey beside him then gave a tiny

croaked a bunny, like a frog!

"Granny!" yelled Pandora. "Their voices are all muddled!" And their *talents* had been mixed-up, too…

The dog wasn't dancing any more, but helter-skeltering like the *snail* had been! And the snail was perched on the rabbit's skateboard and whizzing round the room like a rocket.

"Whoever heard of a *skateboarding snail!*" his owner cried crossly.

"My granny didn't mean it," Pandora muttered. "Un-jamming spells are *so* hard. And she *did* free the guinea-pig that was stuck!"

"Yeah!" groaned the little boy. "But now look – he thinks he's a singing *goldfish*!"

He pointed to his guinea-pig singing opera at the top of his voice.

"*Ombra mai fu di vegetabile!!*"

Pandora blushed. "He's singing it really well, though…"

Quickly, Granny searched through her book for a spell to put everything right. But it was too late. The side door opened and in came the judges for Round Two.

"Clever Clogs time!" the lady judge boomed.

"But—" began Granny. But the judges weren't listening.

"Line up those pets, please. Now!"

Pandora looked around for Cobweb as the
mixed-up pets were lined up.

"Where *is* he?" she said. Pandora couldn't
see him anywhere.

Meanwhile, Granny had found a spell
that should turn all the pets back to
normal. She waved her wand quickly, and
with a huge – BANG! – everything was back
as it should be.

"About time too!" rumbled the snail's owner, still grumpy.

One by one, the pets performed and their special talents were judged. But *still* Pandora couldn't see Cobweb. *Had the magic swirls hit him, and vanished him away!?* she wondered.

Then, just as the judges finished their scoring and were about to announce Best In Show, a little girl pointed to the ceiling and cried, "*Ooo – look!*"

Everyone looked up. And there was Cobweb, three-quarters of the way across the tightrope.

Pandora held her breath. But he wasn't even wobbling. He was great!

71

Cobweb reached the end of the tightrope and bowed, and the judges smiled and nodded. They quickly scribbled something down on their clipboards. Then everyone gathered to find out who had won the show.

"Third…" said the stick-insect judge, standing tall, "is Dexter the dancing dog!" Everyone clapped as Dexter tap-danced up for his rosette.

"And second," he said, "is Holly the hamster! A *very* nice roller-skating action!" Again, everyone clapped as Holly got her frilly rosette.

"And that just leaves first place!" said the lady judge. "And Best In Show goes to…" She paused and Pandora crossed her fingers tightly.

"…Cobweb the cat for his shiny coat and *amazing* tightrope-walking and trapezing!"

As everyone clapped, Granny stepped forward with Cobweb in her arms. But suddenly someone was shouting over the applause…

"Hold on a minute!" It was the owner of Sparky – the helter-skeltering snail.

"*Trazpezing* did you say?" he roared. "Well – I don't remember seeing *ANY trapezing* – he's a fake!"

"No w-wait – he can trapeze!" Granny spluttered.

"Prove it or *lose* it!" cried someone else.

"Right then!" said Granny. She put Cobweb down and jumped on to her broomstick with Pandora.

"Up, broom!" she cried. And as it zoomed into the air, a trapeze tumbled down from the bristles and Cobweb leaped up and caught it.

While Granny soared high above the
crowd, Cobweb did the most
amazing tricks. No one could
say he couldn't trapeze
after this!

As he flew past the judges, the cup was held up and Cobweb scooped it into his paw.

Then Granny looped-the-loop gracefully, before heading to the open door.

"Even *superstars* need their tea!" she called back.

"Bye, then!" Pandora waved.

And clever old Cobweb trapezed ALL the way home!

MUSEUM
MAYHEM!

Chapter One

All week at school, Pandora's class had been learning about different people from the past and how they lived. And now they were going to the museum after school to see the exhibits, and then stay for a special *sleepover*. It was what they'd all been waiting for!

The children and their teacher, Mr Bibble, arrived at the museum just after tea.

Granny had come along too as one of the helpers.

The museum looked really spooky at night. Pandora and her friends couldn't wait to explore. Granny was excited, too. *Bringing History to Life* was the children's topic at school. And *nobody* could bring history to life like *she* could!

81

The class had been put into groups and each went off to a different area. Pandora's group went to see the Vikings first.

"Oh, a longboat!" Granny cried, jumping into it at once. She waved her wand at some Viking dummies sitting at the oars and – bang! – they turned into a REAL Viking crew!

"Right!" roared the leader, Erik Bluetooth. "Anyone else for a voyage? We've got new *lands* to go and find!"

"Yay!" cheered the children. They couldn't miss a Viking adventure!

Climbing in, the children and Granny joined the crew at the oars. Then Granny flicked her wand at the floor and a huge choppy ocean appeared.

"And look – we're wearing Viking *clothes*," cried Pandora. Even Cobweb the cat had a mini-Viking-helmet with horns!

They set sail at once. The waves were enormous.

"*Wicked!*" the children cried.

"But Granny," called Pandora as foam splattered her glasses and the longboat lurched and spun. "What if Mr *Bibble* sees?"

"Then he can be a Viking too, dear!" Granny smiled back.

On they went. Then Jake spotted land. But before they could sail to it…

"*Arggh!*"

A museum attendant had opened the door – only to be met by an *ocean* gushing out into the corridor.

Before the attendant could step inside –
ping! – Pandora magicked the ocean away
and turned everything back to normal. The
attendant marched in. But by now everyone
was standing beside the longboat, back in
normal clothes.

He rubbed his eyes.

"Where's the *water* gone? Oh no – I must
be *seeing* things?!"

Granny looked at Pandora, a puzzled
frown on her face.

"Why not tell him there *were* real
Vikings?" she whispered. After all, the trip
was all about bringing history to life!

"Um, w-where next?" Pandora whispered back. Granny checked her map and her eyes lit up.

"*To the Egyptians!*" cried Granny, marching off. "*What fun!*"

Chapter
Two

The moment they set foot in the Egyptian
room, Granny waved her wand at an
Egyptian coffin and the door slowly opened
– C-R-E-A-K.

"Granny, what are you *doing*?" gasped Pandora. They'd been learning about sarcophagi at school. Inside them were mummies. But not mummies like *parents*. Mummies like dead Egyptian kings!

"Arggh!" screamed the children as the door opened wider. "Run!"

They scattered like ants and hid away. Some dived into big stone urns, others darted behind statues. Pandora's friends dashed into a pyramid, but Pandora stayed put.

"Granny – err, bringing dead Pharaohs to life is probably *not* a good idea."

"No," giggled Granny. "I just wanted a peep inside. I'll close it again if you like?"

Pandora nodded. "Hmmm, I think so. Um – *quick*!"

Granny waved her wand at the coffin and
— *C-R-E-A-K* the door closed again.

"Come out!" Pandora called to her
friends. "The coast is clear!"

Her friends crept out and Pandora explained about the "little mix-up". Then Granny magicked up some Egyptian paper and plant dyes, and some very special-looking pens.

"So, who'd like to try some Egyptian writing?" she asked.

"Yes, please!" cried the children. Hieroglyphics looked really fun!

As the children wrote, Granny turned herself into an Egyptian Pharaoh. But an alive one, not a dead one, so that was fine.

Granny loved all the ancient jewellery she found lying around the place. She liked wearing lots of thick black eye make-up too.

When the children had finished their writing, they tried to work out each other's messages...

97

"No one will guess mine!"
Pandora said. She held up
her message and smiled.

"Easy peasy!" cried
Bluebell, who was great at
hieroglyphics. "That says –
I … love … my … squiggly
granny!"

"Not my *squiggly* granny!" Pandora
snorted. "Those squiggles are just for
decoration!"

"Well, I love you too, dear!" Granny smiled back with a wink.

Now they were going to the Tudor room to meet up with the rest of their class. Granny magicked her normal(ish!) clothes back on, and led everyone out.

"I can't wait for this!" Pandora cried. They'd been learning about the Tudors last week.

"All those gowns – and even Henry the Eighth!" beamed Nellie.

This room would be the best one yet!

Chapter Three

But the Tudor room was dull – dull –
DULL!

There were only two models, wearing
"disappointing" clothes. And on the Tudor
banqueting table were just three plastic
grapes and a pie…

Mr Bibble explained that the Tudor room
was in the middle of having a makeover.
"So lots of the things are missing," he said.

Pandora looked glum. "But, Granny," she whispered, "there's not *even* a Henry the Eighth!"

"That doesn't mean there *can't* be one!" Granny grinned back.

She turned to Mr Bibble. "Don't you worry, dear – if you want history brought to life, I'm the one for the job! A *makeover* you say? Why, I can do that in a jiffy!"

"I-I really don't think—" Mr Bibble began. But it was too late.

Granny's wand was out
and suddenly – *TING!*
– all the children looked
like Tudors!

The girls' gowns were made from the softest silk, and the boys' doublets from the smoothest velvet. There were also knights, and jesters, and musicians with drums, and lutes and tambourines.

Pandora adored her pink silk gown. And as for Mr Bibble, he slowly looked down to see a big round tummy!

Draped around his shoulders was a thick fur cape. On his head was a hat with a feather. And his trousers had gone, and in their place were…

"*Tights?!*" he squeaked. He looked at Granny.

"I'm—"

"Yes, dear!" smiled Granny. "You're Henry the Eighth!"

"Tee hee!" the children giggled. He looked so funny!

Now Granny waved her wand at the
plastic food and a real Tudor banquet
appeared! There was roast goose with
cherries, jam tart shields, and little Tudor
roses made from cream.

"Hooray!" cried the children, tucking
in. And – wow – the food was so yummy!
Why just *read* about a Tudor feast when you
could EAT one instead!

Finally, Mr Bibble called everyone together. It was time to get ready for bed. The sleepover was happening in the Stone Age room, inside a big stone circle. As they walked there, Granny magicked the children's Tudor outfits into Stone Age creature-onesies instead.

"I'm not having one of those!" cried Mr Bibble.

"Then you can stay as Henry!" Granny smiled. "But do stop being such a grouchy old grump … your Highness!"

Chapter
Four

They set up camp inside the stones under a model of a big woolly mammoth. A little way off a model of a sabre tooth tiger bared its long, sharp teeth.

"*This is so exciting!*" the children giggled.

They wriggled into their sleeping bags. But the children weren't tired. And nor was Granny…

"How about I magic up some snap

cards?" she smiled.

"No," said Mr Bibble.

"Or some cocoa?"

"No!" Mr Bibble sounded very firm. "ONE," he snapped, "my tights are too itchy! TWO – you have done *enough* magic! And THREE – I'm tired. *Very* tired!"

"We're not…" groaned the children.

"Too bad!"

Everyone silently settled back down. But *someone* was still feeling chirpy…

"Or, how about we tell spooky stories?" said Granny.

"Shhh!" hissed Mr Bibble. "SLEEP!"

Sighing, Granny shook her head. Sleepovers were meant to be FUN!

"Granny! What are you *doing*?" whispered Pandora as Granny edged out her wand.

"Bringing history to life again!" Granny whispered back with a smile.

She pointed her wand at the sabre tooth tiger and gave it a secret little flick. The tiger blinked, then peered around the room, eyes wide.

"*Granny,*" gasped Pandora, but Granny just winked…

"Don't worry, dear. He won't hurt anyone. The spell made him as gentle as a pussycat! Oh, and as *playful* too – watch this…"

They watched as the sabre tooth tiger now spotted the feather on Mr Bibble's "Henry" hat. The tiger twitched his tail, wiggled his bottom – then off he raced to catch it!

"Rahh!" cried the tiger playfully as he bounded across the room. Mr Bibble saw him.

"Argggh!" he screamed. He scrambled to his feet then pounded to the door, his big round tummy wobbling.

"You can't eat *me*! I'm King Henry the
Eighth I'll have you know!"

Granny let out a giggle. "No, silly! He just wants to *play* – stop running!"

With that, the tiger leaped through the air and landed – *kerr-splatt!* – on Mr Bibble.

He batted the feather with his spade-like
paw. Then out came his floppy wet tongue
and – *SLUUUURRRPPPRP!* – he licked Mr
Bibble on the nose!

"See?" laughed Granny. "He's just a *pussycat*!" And she tickled the tiger under his chin. "Coo-chi-coo!"

The children were now all rolling about. Bringing history to life was such fun!

But *everything* was fun with a certain someone around. "Oh, Granny!" smiled Pandora. "You're the BEST!"

The End